THE QUAIL CLUB

Carolyn Marsden

CANDLEWICK PRESS
CAMBRIDGE, MASSACHUSETTS

I would like to acknowledge Hive members Gretchen Woelfle
and Gretchen Will Mayo for their encouragement and
suggestions and my editors Deborah Wayshak and
Amy Ehrlich, for leading me deeper into the story.

Copyright © 2006 by Carolyn Marsden

First paperback edition 2008

The Library of Congress has cataloged the hardcover edition as follows:

Marsden, Carolyn.
The Quail Club / Carolyn Marsden — 1st ed.
p.   cm.
Summary: Now in fifth grade, Oy wants to do a Thai dance at the
school talent show until Liliandra threatens to kick her out of their
club if they do not perform an American-style skit together.
ISBN 978-0-7636-2635-8 (hardcover)
[1. Identity—Fiction. 2. Thai Americans—Fiction. 3. Friendship—Fiction.
4. Talent shows—Fiction. 5. Clubs—Fiction. 6. Schools—Fiction.]   I. Title.
PZ7.M35135Qua 2006
[Fic]—dc22   2005054284

ISBN 978-0-7636-3422-3 (paperback)

2 4 6 8 10 9 7 5 3 1

Printed in the United States of America

This book was typeset in Perpetua.

Candlewick Press
2067 Massachusetts Avenue
Cambridge, Massachusetts 02140

visit us at www.candlewick.com

For my daughters,
Preeyanutt Manita and Maleeka Vayna,
and for the members of
the Quail Club

❖ ONE ❖

Oy watched her friends' faces as Mrs. Danovitch passed out the bright yellow flyers. The children whispered together and pointed to the words. The flyers couldn't be just announcements of an open house or free teeth-cleaning, or no one would be excited.

Finally, Mrs. Danovitch slipped the yellow paper onto Oy's desk. It was so bright that the black ink seemed to dance off the page: TALENT SHOW!

"This is a special event for fifth graders, boys and girls," said Mrs. Danovitch as she laid down the last copy, in front of Frankie. "Everyone is invited to try out."

Kelly Marie raised her hand. "Could I sing?" Kelly Marie was always humming tunes under her breath.

"You can sing, dance, play an instrument. Whatever you're good at. Just choose one thing."

Oy thought immediately of her Thai dancing. She had a beautiful pink silk dress with gold threads running through the fabric. She knew several short dances that Pak, her dancing teacher, had taught her. Even though Oy now lived in America, she loved to go to the back room of Pak's auto shop on Saturdays to learn Thai dances. There, among the boxes of car oil and packages of wires, Thai music carried Oy back to the country that her family had left when she was five years old. Sometimes dancing made her miss that green land of rubies and elephants.

Oy folded the paper neatly in fourths and tucked it into her pocket.

At recess, the members of the Quail Club gathered in a cluster near the climber.

When Oy approached, Liliandra shouted, "I've already planned what we're going to do! We're all going to dance together like on TV!" She snapped her fingers and wiggled her hips back and forth, her two long black braids swinging with her skinny body.

"Hey, wait a minute," said Hejski. "My cousin's getting married that night. I can't."

"And I'm going to sing 'America the Beautiful,'" Kelly Marie said.

"Maybe you could do both," said Liliandra.

3

"Nope. The flyer says only one thing per person."

"I don't want to be in it at all," said Marisa, straightening the folds of her skirt. "I don't like being onstage."

"Whatever," Liliandra said as she turned her back on everyone. "Oy and me will just dance then."

Oy waited until the others had left before she spoke to Liliandra. "I may not dance with you either," she said, looking down at the concrete pathway. An ant was crossing a crack, carrying a bit of something in its mouth.

"Why not?" asked Liliandra.

Oy put her hands in her jeans pockets and made fists. "I want to do my Thai dance instead."

"Your *Thai* dance?" Liliandra said. "You want to dance alone instead of with me?"

Oy took a step back. Liliandra sounded angry.

"I was only *thinking* about doing the Thai dance," she said, leaning against the climber for support.

Liliandra came so close that Oy could see the little spokes in the brown part of her eyes. "If you don't dance with me, Olivia," she said, using Oy's American name, *Olivia,* like the rubbery black fruit that came in a can, "I will kick you out of the Quail Club."

Oy sucked in her breath. Liliandra *couldn't.*

But she could. She was the boss of the Quail Club. So that was that, as Mrs. Danovitch was fond of saying.

Oy crouched down, closer to the ant, which was still struggling on its journey. She so loved being in the Quail Club that dancing with Liliandra seemed a small price to pay.

"Tomorrow, I'll bring the music and we'll get started," Liliandra announced with her hands on her hips.

Although the Quail Club met at Hejski's house, and although it was Hejski's dad who worked at the agriculture lab and had brought the incubator home from work, Liliandra had chosen the members of the club.

Oy would never forget the day when Liliandra had tapped her on the shoulder and held out a piece of paper that began: *You are invited* . . . At first, Oy thought it was a birthday party invitation. But this seemed even better. *A club* . . . Oy hadn't even known what *quail* meant, but she'd wanted to be part of the group of friends.

Hejski's dad had taken all five of them to an

ice-cream parlor to celebrate the formation of the club. They'd sat at round tables in the sunshine, and Oy had licked her coconut-flavored scoop extra slowly.

Afterward they'd set up the incubator on Hejski's back porch and studied pictures of quail on the Internet. Oy had learned that quail were birds with plumes on their heads.

At the next meeting, Hejski's dad had taken them to Circle J Tack and Feed to pick out the quail eggs. Back home, they'd each lowered two eggs onto the straw. Oy recalled the feel of the smooth ovals in her hand.

She felt extra lucky to be in the club. The others, except for Hejski, spoke Spanish, yet they were still American in a way that Oy was not.

Hejski's family came from Finland, but she too seemed American. She let Liliandra take her pretty yellow hair out of the braids that wound around her head like a crown. She let Liliandra comb it.

Oy still felt Thai.

When Oy told Kun Mere about the club, she'd asked, "When are you going to eat the little birds?"

"Never!" Oy said. "They're pets." She didn't tell her friends the horrible thing that her mother had said.

She couldn't imagine not being part of the club. If Liliandra made her leave, she wouldn't see the quail hatch. But even more important than the quail was the chance to hang out with the other girls. To talk about silly things. To make plans together. To have friends. To be a friend. She hadn't been lonely since the club was formed.

❖ ❖ ❖

The eggs had gestated in the incubator for many days now and were almost ready to hatch. Oy leaned over the warm orange-lit glass box.

Kelly Marie hummed "Away in a Manger," a Christmas song Oy had heard, about the baby Jesus being born in the straw.

"You guys thirsty?" Hejski asked. She mixed the lemonade in a pitcher, the wooden spoon thumping against the sides of the glass. Because it was the hot season, Oy was glad when Hejski added plenty of ice cubes.

On the screen porch, they sipped the lemonade and watched the incubator. Oy shivered from the cold drink and from excitement.

"I have a surprise," said Hejski suddenly. From a brown paper bag, she pulled a box. The lid said WOOD-BURNING KIT. "My dad bought it. We can make our own Quail Club sign."

Hejski unpacked a tool that looked like a water pistol. She plugged the burner cord into

9

the wall socket. Nearby lay a long flat piece of wood. "See, like this." She moved the point of the burner across the wood, making a *Q.* A burnt smell filled the screen porch.

"Your *Q* is too big. The rest isn't going to fit," Liliandra said.

Kelly Marie touched the wood lightly with her fingertip. "Someone should mark it in pencil first."

"That should be Olivia. She has the best handwriting," Marisa said.

"Here, then." Hejski handed Oy a pencil and the board.

Oy pushed her hair behind her ears and began to sketch out the words QUAIL CLUB very neatly, so that all the letters fit. Just for fun, she thought about how fancy the sign would look if she wrote in the swirly letters of the Thai alphabet.

"Now burn it," Marisa said.

The girls leaned close as Oy touched the tip of the tool to the plaque. A wisp of smoke curled up. Oy steadied her hand. As her letters grew thick and black, she thought of how, with each letter, she was burning a permanent spot for herself in the club. As she burned the letters, she thought of how in Thailand there was a special word, *ghler,* for friends who shared something so important together that they became like siblings. Marisa, Kelly Marie, Hejski, and even Liliandra were becoming her *ghler* sisters.

Kun Mere picked up the yellow flyer. "What does it say, Oy?" she asked in Thai. Kun Mere didn't read English.

"It's about a talent show, Kun Mere. The students will show off their special talents."

Kun Mere smiled. "You, little daughter,

have something very special to share. Why don't you practice one of your dances right now?"

It would be hard for Kun Mere to understand about Liliandra and the American dance and how much being in the Quail Club meant. Oy decided not to tell Kun Mere anything yet.

In her room, Oy slowly slipped her pink dress out of the plastic bag. The gold threads of the fabric shone in the dim light. The silk was cool against her skin.

She put the tight skirt on, and Kun Mere helped her pin the two sashes that fastened diagonally across her upper body.

In the living room, Kun Mere turned on the stereo, then sat down on the sofa to watch Oy practice.

The sounds of Thai instruments filled the room: the slippery, bluish notes of the *clui* flute winding in and out of the bouncy notes of the *ranad,* or Thai xylophone.

Oy moved into her dance.

Little Luk clapped her hands. In two years, she would be five. Then Kun Ya, their grandmother, in Thailand, would send Luk a dress and she too would learn to dance.

Just as the music was ending, Kun Pa came in from his job at the restaurant. He kicked off his flip-flops near the door, then bent down to arrange them neatly.

"Do your dance once more, little daughter," he said in Thai. "I don't often get to see you practice."

Kun Mere pushed the button on the stereo and the music began. This time, Luk joined in behind Oy. Oy glanced back to see Luk's face, serious, the flexible fingers of her tiny hands arching backward in classic Thai style.

Oy bent her knees as deeply as she could while keeping her balance. She moved slowly, with her head held high. A soft green light flowed through her.

When Kun Ya had brought the pink dress from Thailand, she'd dressed Oy in it, leaning over her and gently fastening the sashes. Whenever Oy danced, she remembered those moments with Kun Ya and missed her.

Kun Mere and Kun Pa smiled slightly and leaned forward on the sofa. Even here in America, they expected her to speak Thai, to eat Thai food, to be Thai.

They expected her to do a Thai dance for the talent show. How could she ever explain that she would not?

❖ TWO ❖

Kun Pa climbed in behind the wheel of the old
rust-colored station wagon that he'd bought
from one of the restaurant workers.

"Don't forget to put Luk in the car seat,"
Oy reminded Kun Mere.

Kun Mere used to hold Luk on her lap as
they rode. But after Oy had seen the video at
school about safety belts and car seats, she'd
told Kun Mere that Luk needed a car seat.
"She's safer with me," said Kun Mere at first,

setting her face. But Oy had won the battle: Luk was now locked in.

As they rode across town to the Thai temple, Oy watched the chain of plastic jasmine flowers jiggle from the rearview mirror.

Finally, Kun Pa parked in front of the temple. The *wat* here in America looked nothing like those in Thailand, which were made of gold and decorated with real jewels. This *wat* was just a regular house in a neighborhood.

Even so, the minute Oy stepped inside, she felt as though she was in Thailand. No one had turned on the air conditioning, so the air felt sticky and close, just like in Thailand. Next to shelves for shoes was a sign in the Thai alphabet: WELCOME. PLEASE REMOVE YOUR SHOES. Everyone spoke Thai. *"Sawasdee,"* adults greeted each other, pressing their hands together in front of their chests and bowing.

Oy inhaled the smells of basil and fish sauce, curries and coconut milk, the spicy scent of incense unwinding from the altar.

She held Luk's hand as they approached the monks seated in a row on a platform. Each wore a bright orange robe and had his head shaved. The monks chanted in unison, their eyes downcast. Luk wanted to make the offering: a pack of Ivory soap bars. Already the monks had received golden yellow bath towels; a big package of toilet paper; and paper bills, ones and fives, pinned to a small tree. Oy dropped to her knees and bowed so low that her forehead touched the floor. She peeked to see that Luk was also bowing to the monks and to the huge golden Buddha who stared down with sharp black eyes.

Kun Pa joined the men who were watching Thai TV, brought in through the satellite dish on the roof.

17

Kun Mere had gone to the kitchen with the other women who were preparing the food for the monks. She arranged wedges of watermelon and slices of mango on a platter. Next to her, a woman broke off hunks of sticky rice with her fingers, her soft gold bracelets jangling together. The women kept up their chatter in spite of the monks' steady chanting, piped in through a speaker.

Pak, Oy's dancing teacher, swept in with a silver bowl full of sweet white soup with curls of green coconut gelatin. She winked at Oy, then handed her the dessert soup. "Take it to the monks, little daughter," Pak said.

As Oy set the bowl down on the monks' eating mat, she thought of the bird refuge that her class had visited on a field trip. In the refuge, the birds could eat and drink and bathe without having to worry.

It was the same way here at the temple. Every Sunday morning, she could relax, comfortable in the Thai customs and manners, never having to worry about fitting in with Americans.

At the temple, everyone left American lives behind. Even the American husbands acted Thai, sitting on the floor to eat, greeting others with pressed-together hands and a *"Sawasdee."* Most had met their wives while they were soldiers stationed in Thailand. They happily imitated the customs of their Thai wives.

Oy had heard these women referred to as Thai Americans. She wondered how they had gotten to be called that. She wondered if she was a Thai American yet or if she was still only Thai.

Two boys played a game on the monks' computer. The cartoon figures shot laser guns, aiming zigzaggy fire at each other. Maybe doing American things made a person more of an American. If so, would doing the American dance with Liliandra help? If she did the Thai dance instead, she might never become a Thai American.

Oy went outside to the garden filled with bamboo, lemon grass, mint, and chili plants. Water trickled down the sides of a fountain.

Even out here, Oy could hear the monks' chanting. Usually, no one paid special attention to the chants. Unless people were in the same room as the monks, they went about their business. Today, Oy sat on a bench and tried to listen closely to the wise words of the Buddha.

But her mind couldn't rest. It kept returning to the talent show. What would Liliandra's music sound like? Would Liliandra be happy with the way she danced?

Sometime, she'd have to tell Kun Mere and Kun Pa about Liliandra's dance.

Oy suddenly wished that the talent show had never been announced at all. Instead of being fun, it was only causing problems.

◆ THREE ◆

The next day, when the class entered the room after morning bell, Oy saw Liliandra's boom box underneath her desk.

Liliandra waved a CD from across the room. *You Got Me Down* was written in streaky letters across it.

Seeing the boom box and the CD made Oy feel as though she were at the top of the water slide at Bubba's Slip 'n' Swirl. Once she started down that slide, carried along by gravity and the slick film of water, there was no stopping.

She went to her seat. She opened her binder and began the board assignment, writing a sentence with exactly thirteen words that contained the words *angel, perfect, shadow,* and *shy.* Her pencil was sharpened to a fine tip.

Frankie caught her eye from across the room. He pointed to the words on the board, then at Mrs. Danovitch. Near the side of his head, he drew a circle in the air with his fingertip and laughed silently.

Oy had learned that the gesture meant a person was crazy. She smiled at Frankie. He'd gotten a new haircut, and his hair was short all over except for a tuft that rose above his forehead.

Mrs. Danovitch handed out library books on the solar system. A slim volume landed on Oy's desk with a slap. The cover pictured planets hanging against a background of stars.

"Don't forget that your solar system reports are due soon," said Mrs. Danovitch.

Several people groaned, but Oy liked studying the solar system. It contained both America and Thailand and was a place equally unknown to everyone. When she imagined being on Jupiter, the difference between her country and America seemed small.

The thunderheads had risen early in the morning and hung like fluffy crowns over the mountains. By recess, the clouds had begun to float out over the city, flattening and losing their bunchy shapes.

"Come on, Olivia," shouted Liliandra.

"What's taking you so long?" She carried the boom box and the glittering CD.

Oy followed her to the ramada, where Liliandra slipped the CD into the player. A song came on—rough and wild with a girl singing so fast that Oy could barely make out the words.

"Stand behind and follow me," Liliandra commanded.

Oy stepped into place. Disobeying Liliandra would have felt like going against Mrs. Danovitch, or even her parents. Besides, the music sounded fun, like pinwheels spinning quickly in a breeze.

Liliandra made up the dance as she went along, singing the tune to "You Got Me Down and It Ain't No Use" very loudly and with no melody. Imitating her, Oy twirled her wrists, turned around, and dropped quickly into deep lunges. At the very end, they both lifted their arms high and swiveled their hips in unison.

Oy wasn't used to so much bouncing and turning. Liliandra's dance made her feel like a bottle of bubbly soda when the top is unscrewed.

❖ FOUR ❖

On her way home, Oy stopped in at Jerry's Lee Ho Market, which was owned by Frankie's family.

The ceiling of the market was high, the light dim, the dusty shelves stacked with cans and bottles. Even on the hottest days, the market felt nice inside. The cooler of fresh vegetables, with its fluorescent light white in the gloom, hummed gently.

Yeh-Yeh, Frankie's Chinese grandfather, sat on a high stool behind the counter. His face was completely round, his skin like tracing paper. His eyes looked almost closed, the slits were so narrow.

"Good afternoon." Oy bowed her head slightly to Yeh-Yeh. "Is Frankie here?" she asked quietly. Everything in the market felt hushed.

Yeh-Yeh turned toward the back room and called out in Chinese.

Frankie pushed aside the curtain, then smiled when he saw Oy. He opened the door of the drink cooler and pulled two cans of soda loose from the six-pack wrapping.

He gestured to Oy and lifted the curtain again. They went into the back room of the market. Oy felt lucky to go where no customers were invited. It was like going into the restaurant kitchen where Kun Pa worked. In the kitchen, the real life happened—everything out front was just for customers. When you asked someone out front how they were, they always said, "Fine." In back, people told the truth. The kitchen was lively with stories and jokes.

Frankie pushed aside a messy pile of Chinese newspapers resting on the table. On one wall, a round cooking wok hung on a nail above a hot plate. A fat Chinese Buddha sat on an altar surrounded by red silk flowers. Coins threaded on a red string dangled from the doorknob.

"What's up?" asked Frankie.

"Nothing much," Oy said, popping the tab on her soda.

"Looks like you're going to be in the talent show. I saw you dancing with Liliandra. The dance looked cool."

"Yeah, kind of cool." She wondered if Frankie would understand her problem. "Are you going to be in the talent show?"

"Me?" Frankie pointed toward his chest. "I don't have a talent."

"You play soccer."

"That's not the kind of thing people do in a talent show."

Oy laughed to think of Frankie kicking a ball across the stage. She turned her soda around and around on the table. The skin of water on the outside broke and ran where her fingers touched it, then formed again.

Oy took a long drink, letting the soda bubbles tickle the back of her throat. "I've got a problem," she said at last.

Frankie lifted his eyebrows.

"The problem is that I want to do my Thai dance. And my parents want me to do it."

"So?"

"Liliandra says that if I don't dance with her, I can't be in the Quail Club anymore."

"And you really like the Quail Club?"

Oy nodded. No words could tell how much she liked it.

Frankie bent to pick up a candy wrapper from underneath his chair. "Better tell your parents, then."

"But they'll be so sad."

"They've got to learn, Oy. You're in America now. Yeh-Yeh"—he jerked his head in the direction of the other room—"doesn't expect me to do tai chi."

"Thai what?"

"It's an old Chinese martial art where you move really slow. He knows I want to play soccer instead. The same way you want to do an American dance." Frankie scrunched up the candy wrapper and aimed it toward the trash can. He made the shot.

31

Then, from his pocket, he took a bag of Sour Balz and handed it to Oy. "You're an American, so here's some American candies to remind you."

Oy put the bag in the outer pocket of her backpack. She began to pull the zipper closed, then stopped and smiled. Frankie had called her an American.

"Americans eat everything," Frankie continued. "Would you like a Chinese moon cake?" He opened a cupboard to reveal round buns. "Or spicy Mexican candy?" From his shirt pocket, Frankie took a brightly wrapped treat.

"I'll try a little of each," Oy said.

❖ FIVE ❖

Kun Mere was ironing the family clothes, the space between her eyebrows pinched in concentration.

Oy sat close by, on the sofa, working on her solar system report, copying her notes in small, neat cursive. From time to time, she glanced up at Kun Mere.

"You don't have to iron my T-shirts, Kun Mere," she finally said.

"They are very wrinkled."

"That's okay. Everyone's school clothes are wrinkled."

But Kun Mere set her mouth in a tight crease and continued to iron each piece of clothing in the basket, including the T-shirts, and even underwear.

Oy finished copying, then opened her science book to the chapter on the solar system. Each planet orbited the sun in its own pathway except for Pluto, which swung into the pathway of Neptune. Pluto was like Liliandra, Oy thought, always interfering with others.

Oy drew the planets one by one, on nine separate sheets of paper.

Kun Pa came home just as Kun Mere finished her basket of ironing and Oy her drawing. He sat down on the couch beside Oy and listened to her read the report. He ran his finger lightly over the planets drawn with pale colored pencils.

Oy had to read aloud to Kun Pa because he didn't read American cursive. She'd tried to teach him cursive, using handwriting worksheets from third grade. But Kun Pa wasn't a good student. "I already can read American print," he said. "That's enough for me."

But I'm learning new things all the time, Oy had wanted to say.

Now she read to him about Mercury running swiftly close to the sun and about Neptune's atmosphere, deliciously sea green but deadly.

"Excellent," he said when she'd finished.

"Thank you, Kun Pa." Oy was proud of the way she always got high marks in school. Her handwriting was prettier than anyone's in her class. She moved closer to Kun Pa until their bare feet rested side by side.

"At school, we're going to have a talent show. Kids can sing or dance or play piano or do whatever they're good at."

Kun Pa nodded. "And you are good at dancing."

"Yes," Oy said slowly. But it wasn't that simple. How could she explain how complicated the talent show had become? "A girl wants me to be in an American dance with her. I want to dance my Thai dance. I just don't know what to do." She didn't tell him Liliandra's threat about the Quail Club.

Kun Pa sat very still, his hands folded on top of Oy's report.

"I may do the American dance instead of my Thai dance," she finished. Her voice sounded firmer than she'd expected.

Kun Pa sat with Oy's report on his lap, the planets tilting across his knees. "But your Thai dance is your heritage," he said.

Oy suddenly felt confused. Kun Pa didn't understand. To do her Thai dance, she'd have

36

to stand up against Liliandra and tell her no. Yet Kun Pa himself had taught her always to be polite and never hurt a friend's feelings, no matter what. In Thai, being careful not to offend others was called *krain jai*. "Liliandra, the girl who's in charge, would be upset if I left the dance."

"It would be an honor for you to dance the Thai dance," Kun Pa said as though he hadn't listened to her.

Kun Mere was chopping vegetables, bringing her knife down hard on the cutting board, working as though she overheard nothing.

Oy sighed. Her family would never understand. Kun Pa spent all his time with other Thai people at the Lotus Blossom. Kun Mere hardly left the house. Luk was still a little kid. Only Oy seemed to struggle with American problems.

"I want to be in the talent show with my friend." Oy kept her head bowed slightly so she wouldn't seem disrespectful.

"But you can do a dance that no one else can do. It would be special for the audience to see something different." Kun Pa closed the report folder.

Even though she sat close to Kun Pa, Oy felt as though she was drifting away from him. She linked her arm with his, feeling his warm skin against her forearm.

"Do what makes you happy, Oy." After a while, Kun Pa added, "You've become an American so fast."

Oy held Kun Pa's elbow tightly against her own. Suddenly, she longed to sit in his lap as she had when she was small. And yet by choosing the American dance, she'd moved further away from him. She'd become a little less Thai.

"I'll be dancing at Songkran soon anyway," she reminded him. She always danced for Thai New Year.

"That's true, little daughter," Kun Pa agreed.

"Will you come to the talent show if I dance the American dance?" Oy asked softly. Waiting for the answer, she held her whole body still.

Kun Pa looked toward Kun Mere, across the room, as though to seek her advice. But she was dropping the vegetables into a pan of hot oil.

Kun Pa tightened his arm against hers. "Of course. We will all come."

❖ SIX ❖

One of the chicks had already hatched, leaving the tiny eggshell in tatters.

With a disposable camera, Marisa took photos of the wet chick. "Oooh," she squealed. "So cute."

"I don't think it's cute," said Kelly Marie, moving away from the incubator.

"It will be," Hejski insisted. She clutched a thin book called *Raising Wild Fowl.*

Liliandra took the rubber band off her

ponytail and shook her hair loose. "That's gonna take a long time."

"Don't you remember about the ugly duckling that turned into a swan?" Marisa asked.

"That ain't no swan," Liliandra insisted.

The chick looked like one of the pompoms on Marisa's shoelaces, Oy thought. She didn't mind that it wasn't as fluffy as she'd expected. "May I hold it?" She stepped closer.

"Not yet," said Liliandra. "Hejski's book says not yet."

To celebrate the hatching, Oy held open the bag of Frankie's Sour Balz. Hejski chose a green one, Marisa yellow, Kelly Marie pink. Liliandra was the last to choose. Her hand hovered over the bag. At last she darted her thumb and index finger inside and snatched up Oy's favorite—purple. It was the only purple. Oy took white instead.

Now everyone had one cheek pooched

out with a candy. The sourness made the skin pucker inside Oy's cheek. She shifted the piece of candy from one side of her mouth to the other.

Two more chicks began to break out of their shells.

Hejski's dad sat down on the nearby lawn chair, propping his feet up on the low table. Oy looked away. The first time she'd seen him present his feet not only to her and the other girls, but to the Buddha and heavens above as well, she'd stared in astonishment. Thai people tucked their feet carefully away from others.

She was to call him Yuri, Oy reminded herself. In Thailand, she would have called her friend's father Kun Loong, "Uncle," or even Kun Pa, "Father," if her family knew him well. But in America, he was Yuri.

Hejski turned on the lights in the screen porch.

Oy called home. "Kun Mere, is it all right if I'm a little late? The quail are still hatching." She used the English word *quail,* not knowing the word in Thai.

"And your homework? When will you do your homework?"

Oy sighed. Her mother would never learn that there were some things more important than school.

"I don't have much tonight, Kun Mere. I'll get it done."

After she hung up, Marisa, who was waiting to use the phone, covered her mouth, as though not to laugh. "Is that Chinese you were speaking?"

Oy laughed quickly. Kids always teased her when she spoke Thai to her parents.

Marisa began to speak to her mother in Spanish.

Oy thought about saying, *Was that Russian*

you were speaking? but the joke didn't really seem funny.

When the chicks were settled in the straw, basking in the warmth of the incubator lamp, Yuri drove everyone home. He turned the radio high, to a rock 'n' roll station. In the back seat, Oy bumped shoulders with Marisa and Hejski as they swayed to the music and sang along. Marisa took Oy's hand, and Oy took Hejski's, until they were all linked together, bumping shoulders and giggling. In the front seat, Kelly Marie and Liliandra sang along with Yuri. Oy smiled. It was fun to join in with American friends.

But as Yuri drove close to her house, Oy swayed less and sang more softly. When Yuri pulled into her driveway, Oy jumped out quickly, slamming the car door, barely thanking him. She didn't want her parents to hear the unfamiliar American music.

❖ SEVEN ❖

Oy tried to hide her food from Liliandra, making a circle around it by resting her forearms on the table.

"What's that?" Liliandra asked anyway, leaning over.

Kun Mere had packed sticky rice into a banana leaf packet. In the center of the treat was a sweet paste of mung beans.

"It's my lunch," Oy answered. Usually, she ate school lunch, but today, Kun Mere had had no change for lunch money.

"But what *is* it?"

"Rice."

"Like normal rice?"

"It's sticky rice cooked in a special pot."

"Sticky? I like Uncle Ben's Minute Rice 'cause it's fluffy. How come the rice is in the leaf thing? Doesn't your mom have plastic wrap?"

"The leaf makes the rice taste good," Oy explained.

"Jeez. Learn something new every day." Liliandra tore the crust off her grilled cheese sandwich. "And speaking of new, I saw the coolest new dancing on TV last night. Channel 13. You see it?"

Oy was about to take a bite of sticky rice but stopped. She shook her head. At her house, the TV was covered with a drape of Thai silk.

"Don't say you don't watch TV," said Liliandra, sniffing her sandwich.

"Not much," Oy admitted. Although Kun Pa wished he had a satellite to bring in TV from Thailand, it was too expensive. American TV wasn't worth looking at. The TV was used only to watch the videos from Thailand and India that Kun Pa and other workers at the restaurant shared among themselves.

"Then you've never seen dancing on TV?" Liliandra asked, laying the sandwich on the cafeteria tray.

Oy shook her head again. She shielded her Thai lunch with both hands.

Liliandra opened her eyes wide. "You gotta come over to my house, then, and see some TV. You gotta get some ideas."

The next afternoon, Oy walked home with Liliandra. "I'll be doing homework with my friend," she'd told Kun Mere without looking

her in the eye. Yet the lie wasn't a big one.
The talent show was for school, after all.

Liliandra led the way across a busy street.

Oy looked in both directions several times.
She felt as if she was stepping off the curb into
a new world. She was going to Liliandra's
house.

Several blocks later, they arrived at a small
yellow house. Liliandra pulled a key from her
jeans pocket, fitted it into the lock, and turned
it. The door swung open.

Oy wondered why Liliandra didn't just
walk in. Kun Mere was always waiting for her
to come home from school. Sometimes she
even sat with Luk on the front steps, waiting.

Then she realized that no one was home.
"Where's your mom?" she asked.

"Working."

"Your dad?"

Liliandra shrugged. "He's away."

Oy had never been in a house without a grownup before. Anything could happen. She began to slip off her shoes, then saw that Liliandra kept hers on. At Hejski's, people also wore shoes in the house.

"I'm starved," declared Liliandra. "That school lunch was disgusting."

Oy felt hungry too. At home, Kun Mere always had a plate of sliced pineapple or mango ready for her.

Liliandra marched to the kitchen and opened the refrigerator.

Oy peeked over Liliandra's shoulder to see a can of Coke, a head of lettuce, and slices of orange cheese.

"Here," said Liliandra, pulling out the cheese. "We can eat this. Not the Coke. That's my mom's." She passed Oy a slice of cheese.

49

When Oy bit it, she realized it was wrapped in thin plastic. She peeled the plastic off. The cheese had almost no taste. She might as well have eaten the plastic wrap.

"And now," said Liliandra, picking up a remote. She pushed a button and the TV came on. She flicked through the channels and then stopped. "Here we go."

A song that sounded like "You Got Me Down" was playing. A girl danced in a bikini top and a skirt so short it barely hid her underwear. When she twisted her hips, the diamond in her bellybutton flashed.

Liliandra began to dance and sing along.

Six more dancing girls came up behind the TV girl. Their tops were skin-colored, so it looked as if they had nothing on at all.

Oy blinked. She'd never seen this kind of dancing before. Had never imagined it, even.

The girl sang a new song about her heart getting broken. The screen behind her flashed pictures of swords chopping up red Valentine hearts.

Oy plunked herself down onto the couch. It would be too embarrassing to dance like those girls. Did Liliandra really expect her to do that?

Suddenly, Liliandra left the room. She returned with a large book that looked like a photo album. "I have something to show you." She sat down next to Oy, the couch dipping under her weight, and opened the book.

Inside were pages of postage stamps laid out in neat rows.

"My dad gave me this album. He's in the army, and when he travels around, he collects stamps. He gives me the ones he has two of."

As Liliandra turned the pages, Oy saw

51

miniature pictures of birds, flowers, buildings, and people who looked like presidents and kings.

Every now and then she took peeks at the dancing girls on the TV. She didn't want Liliandra to know she was peeking at them. She didn't want her to know how shocked she was.

"This stamp is from France"—Liliandra put her finger on a small green rectangle—"and this is from Kuwait." She touched a reddish orange one.

"Where's that?"

"Africa." Liliandra sat up straighter.

"Do you have any from Thailand?"

"Yes, I have three from Taiwan." She flipped the pages and pointed.

Oy peered at the tiny squares. "That's China," she said, "not Thailand."

"Taiwan. Thailand. Whatever." Liliandra flicked her wrist.

Oy looked around. "Is your dad not here because he's in the military?"

"Yeah." Liliandra stared ahead at nothing. Then she crossed the room, picked up a photo in a gold frame, and brought it to Oy. "This is a picture of him."

Oy looked closely at the man in a soldier's uniform.

Liliandra touched the glass over the face, then wiped off the dust with the cuff of her shirt. "He's gone too much." Suddenly, she laid the photo face-down on the table.

"Is he always gone?" Oy asked.

"He's mostly gone."

"Oh." Oy couldn't imagine Kun Pa being away. "Isn't that sad for you?"

"Yes, it kind of is." The dancing came to an end and Liliandra shut off the TV. She propped her chin in her hand, her elbow on the arm of the couch. "But I'm used to it."

❖ ❖ ❖

That night, Oy waited until Kun Mere put Luk to bed, singing a Thai lullaby: "Hush, little elephant. Hush, little snake. . . ." Then she flipped through the channels with the remote control, just as Liliandra had. There was news of a bank holdup, a cartoon of two rabbits being chased by a giraffe, a game show with a huge spinning wheel.

Suddenly, she hit channel 13 and the dancing girls filled the screen. Oy kept her finger on the OFF button of the remote. This time the girls wore tiger masks and short dresses made of animal skins. Every now and then, in the middle of a line of song, they lifted the masks and snarled.

Oy turned off the TV, feeling embarrassed for the Buddha who gazed from his altar mounted on the opposite wall.

❖ EIGHT ❖

It was Saturday afternoon and Liliandra was coming over to practice the dance.

"It's your turn now," she'd declared. "I'll be at your house after lunch."

Oy could think of no reason to say no.

Kun Mere had made *tom kha,* Oy's favorite coconut chicken soup.

The fragrant steam rose into her face, yet Oy sat without touching the bowl.

"What is the matter, little daughter?" Kun Mere asked.

"I've never had Liliandra over before, Kun Mere. I don't feel like eating."

"Is there something to be worried about?"

She couldn't explain to Kun Mere. If Liliandra thought her house was too weird or that her family was too weird, she wouldn't want to be friends. And if she didn't want to be a friend, neither might the other girls. Oy stared down at the bright red peppers bobbing in the soup.

Kun Mere touched Oy's hand. "Why don't you go take the broom and sweep? That will calm you down. Then you can eat."

Oy got the broom from the closet by the stove. She went outside and swept the leaves and dirt from the front steps, then the path. She swept the steps again and was starting on the path again when Kun Mere called, "Come eat your soup, Oy. I warmed it up."

Oy ate only the mushrooms shaped like tiny Chinese hats.

A durian fruit sat on the counter like a spiky football or a soldier's grenade. Surely, Kun Mere wouldn't serve *that*. It smelled so strong that even some Thai people refused to eat it.

A knock came on the door.

Oy tucked Luk's old baby blanket under a sofa cushion, then opened the door to Liliandra.

Liliandra carried her big black boom box. With her free hand, she pointed to the row of shoes outside the front door. "What's with that?"

"We take off our shoes before we go inside."

"Me too?"

Oy wanted to beckon to Liliandra—*Come on in like you are*—since Americans wore

57

their shoes everywhere, but Kun Mere would be upset. "You too," she said.

When Liliandra knelt down to untie her sneakers, Oy unclasped her hands.

Kun Mere came to the doorway with Luk hiding behind her legs. She spoke in Thai, "Tell your friend welcome, little daughter."

When Kun Mere went into the kitchen, Liliandra whispered, "I don't get how you and your mom talk like that. How do you understand each other?"

"We're used to it." Oy shrugged, yet wished once again that Kun Mere would learn English.

Then Liliandra stared at the altar where the Buddha sat, the incense smoke uncurling over his face. "That smoke smells better than cigarettes."

She turned to the other wall. "Who's that?"

she asked loudly, pointing at two framed pictures opposite the Buddha.

"The king and queen of Thailand." The king was dressed in a formal white coat, the queen in a green evening dress.

"Oooh, they have a king and queen there? But where's their crowns?"

"They don't have crowns."

"If I was a queen, I'd wear one."

It was true, Oy thought. Other kings and queens did wear crowns. Why not these?

Just then, Oy smelled the durian. She could hear Kun Mere using her big knife to hack it apart. Oh, why had Kun Mere opened *that*! Didn't she *know*?

Just as Oy had feared, Liliandra sniffed and said, "What stinks?"

"That's a fruit."

"A *fruit*? It smells like rotten eggs."

"It tastes good though. It's my favorite."

59

"It'll never be mine." Liliandra pinched her nose closed.

Oy took tiny breaths, pretending to herself that the durian didn't smell as bad as it did.

Kun Mere gave Oy a plate of coconut balls, then handed Liliandra two glasses of water with slices of lemon floating in the ice.

On the counter sat a bowl filled with golden pillows of durian fruit. Oy looked away from it.

"We'll eat in the backyard," Oy said to Kun Mere.

Oy led Liliandra outside to sit on the back steps, in the fresh air.

Liliandra picked up one of the coconut treats between her thumb and forefinger. She touched her tongue to it, her eyes crossing in an effort to watch, before popping it into her mouth.

Oy watched. Would Liliandra make a face? Would she look confused?

Liliandra smiled. "Mmm, mmm," she said, chewing. "Your mom make these?"

Oy smiled too. "Yes, she makes lots of good things. She uses the spices over there." Oy gestured toward Kun Mere's garden of lemon grass and chilies, bamboo and tropical plants with white stripes on the leaves.

"My mom mostly gets takeout."

Luk opened the door and held the bowl of durian.

Even outside, Oy could smell the strong odor. "Put it here, Luk," she said, patting the step beside her, on the other side from Liliandra.

Luk sat down and took a golden pillow in both hands. She took a big bite, smearing the yellow custard on her cheeks.

"How can she eat that stuff?" whispered Liliandra.

Oy hoped that the breeze was carrying the

smell away from Liliandra. "It doesn't taste like it smells."

Liliandra rolled her eyes.

She had to get Liliandra thinking about something else. "What are we going to wear?" she asked, remembering the tiny outfits the girls had worn on TV. A shiver—cold like ice cream, hot like Kun Mere's curry sauce—ran through her. Kun Mere, who refused to wear even a sleeveless blouse, would never sew her clothes that showed so much of her body.

"Jeans and tank tops."

"Only that?" Oy asked. And yet she was relieved. No animal mask or leopard-skin bikini.

"We'll look good. Besides, my mom doesn't have money for a costume."

When they'd finished the plate of snacks, Oy said, "Let's practice out here." She didn't want Liliandra to smell the durian inside. She might go back and tell the whole Quail Club that Oy's house stank.

"But I don't have any shoes. They're on your front porch."

"The grass is soft," Oy said. She led the way to the other side of the orange tree, and Liliandra slid the CD into the boom box. When Liliandra wasn't looking, Oy turned the volume knob down a little.

They kicked and turned and knelt on one knee. They twirled and lifted their arms overhead.

When they practiced for the second time, Liliandra turned the volume way up.

Oy glanced toward the house. Was the American music too loud? Was Kun Mere listening?

Luk joined in, swiveling her hips and snapping her tiny fingers.

Suddenly, the back door opened. Kun Mere came out and down the back steps. Without saying a word, she took Luk by the hand and led her inside.

Oy stopped dancing. Why had Kun Mere taken Luk away? Was it because—suddenly Oy's stomach felt quivery—she and Liliandra *did* look like the girls on TV?

"What's wrong?" Liliandra asked.

"We've practiced enough. We'd better stop now."

"But we're just getting started." Liliandra turned on the music again.

As Oy danced, she saw Kun Mere's face at the window. She didn't look happy. Would Kun Mere come out and take *her* by the hand too? Then Liliandra wouldn't be happy. Oy's stomach quivered again.

❖ NINE ❖

When Liliandra's mother drove up to get her, she didn't come in. Instead, she honked the horn and Liliandra ran out, calling, "See ya tomorrow."

Then, with her hand on the door handle of the car, she said, "I had fun."

The words sailed through the air.

Oy shouted back, "I had fun too." She was smiling even after Liliandra's car had turned the corner.

Kun Mere sat on the couch, sewing a button on Luk's blue blouse. She caught Oy's eyes and glanced at the spot on the couch beside her.

Oy sat down. Liliandra had enjoyed herself, but Kun Mere had taken Luk away. She folded her hands in her lap and waited.

Kun Mere poked the needle through the hole of the button and pulled the thread through. "What kind of dancing were you and your friend doing, little daughter?" she asked at last.

"American dancing, Kun Mere."

"Not American dancing like the kind they do in squares."

"No. Not that kind." Oy almost laughed. She'd seen people square dancing at the neighborhood center, the women wearing skirts like bells. "This is kids' dancing."

"Is this kids' dancing what you want to do for the school show?"

"Yes, Kun Mere."

Kun Mere looped the blue thread through the holes three more times, yanking it tight, before she said, "Dancing and music like that are not appropriate for young girls."

Oy looked down at her bare feet. How could Kun Mere say what was appropriate? She hardly knew anything about American ways. She felt like telling Kun Mere what Americans thought of durian, how stinky it was, how embarrassing. Instead, she bowed her head slightly and said, "Yes, Kun Mere."

Oy sank back into the couch cushions. Would Kun Mere never ever learn about America?

Luk climbed onto the couch and nestled into Oy's lap.

Oy pulled her close in a hug. Luk was innocent now, but someday would also have to make these hard decisions.

Kun Mere finished sewing the button, knotted the thread, and cut it off neatly. She tugged on the remaining buttons, found a loose one, and began to sew it tight.

Luk fell asleep, snoring lightly against Oy's chest.

Oy watched Kun Mere knot the thread again and cut it. Kun Mere put the needle and thread away in her wooden box, then folded Luk's blouse.

Oy didn't like what Kun Mere had said about the dancing. But she had to admit that whenever she'd practiced the American dance, she hadn't felt like herself. She'd been copying Liliandra, and without knowing it, the girls on TV.

Kun Mere had merely voiced what her

own heart had already told her. Kun Mere had made Oy's own choice clear.

Oy eased Luk onto the couch. She got up and carried the phone into her room. From her desk drawer, she took the tiny phone book listing the numbers of the members of the Quail Club. The book was pale green silk with lotus flowers on the cover, a gift from Kun Ya. Oy ran her finger down the list to Liliandra's name and number.

And then she paused. In spite of the durian, Liliandra had enjoyed being at her house. At the end, she'd been friendly, nicer than she'd ever been.

Yet Oy had made her decision.

Liliandra wasn't going to like her quitting. It would make her so mad that she would kick her out of the Quail Club. Oy would never see the chicks get bigger, would never hold one. And even worse, she would no

69

longer be friends with the girls listed on the page of the small green book.

Oy wiped her tears with her sleeve.

Finally, she dialed Liliandra's number.

Liliandra herself answered the phone. She sounded very young and not at all bossy. Oy wondered if Liliandra's mother had dropped her off and gone to work, leaving Liliandra home by herself.

Oy's hand was so sweaty that she had to hold the receiver tightly.

"Hey, I never got a call from you before," said Liliandra.

"I know," Oy said, staring down at her knees.

"What's up?"

Oy squeezed her eyes shut. "Liliandra, I've decided to do my own dance after all."

Liliandra said nothing. The silence was as deep and black as the night outside the window.

Oy held the phone away to make sure that the ON light was still glowing green.

Finally, Liliandra said, "It's your mom, isn't it, that makes you want to do that dance instead of mine."

"In a way, yes. But I want to too. I don't get a chance to dance it often." She couldn't tell Liliandra about what Kun Mere had said.

"Whatever. I gotta go now."

"Wait," Oy said, not wanting to hang up yet. "Are you all by yourself?"

"Yeah. My mom had to go back to work."

"Aren't you scared?"

"Nope," Liliandra said, and Oy imagined her tossing her braids over her shoulders. But then she added, "Just a little when the sun goes down."

Oy couldn't think of anything to say. She'd never been alone in a house, much less at night.

71

"Gotta go," Liliandra said, then hung up.

Oy stayed in the chair, imagining Liliandra by herself with the darkness pressing in from all sides. She shivered and set the phone down.

Then she thought of the Quail Club. Liliandra hadn't mentioned kicking her out, but she wouldn't forget.

❖ TEN ❖

It was April Fool's Day, and Mrs. Danovitch's class had a sub named Mr. T.

"I bet Mrs. Danovitch got such a bad April Fool's joke played on her that she couldn't make it to school," whispered Kelly Marie loudly.

When Frankie coughed twice, everyone in the class dropped a pencil. That joke had been planned for Mrs. Danovitch, but it worked for Mr. T too. He got down on his knees to look at the floor, his forehead furrowed into many tiny lines.

In Thailand, children prepared special flower arrangements for their teachers. Here in America, Oy dropped her pencil along with the others.

Just as Mr. T was getting up, Liliandra said, "Teacher, there's a butterfly on your shoulder," and Mr. T actually looked.

Oy laughed along with the others.

The recess bell rang, and as Mr. T called the tables, the class got into line.

Frankie bounced the soccer ball into the air, hitting it with his forearms as he lined up.

Mr. T made him go back to his seat and start all over again.

Outside, the line scattered. Frankie ran to play soccer. Marisa and Kelly Marie strolled toward the climber, their heads bent close as though they shared a secret. Maybe Marisa was going to join Kelly Marie in singing "America the Beautiful." Hejski went to the library to do research on quail.

Oy climbed to the top of the climber and perched on a bar, swinging her legs.

Below her, under the ramada, she saw Liliandra sitting on the ground with her knees pulled up, her forehead pressed against them. She didn't move, even though Frankie and his soccer team ran close to her. She looked different from the girl who'd danced so crazy, snapping her fingers. All Liliandra's energy—spicy hot like Kun Mere's chilies—had disappeared.

Oy had a sudden thought that made her almost lose her balance. Had it been her phone call that made Liliandra sit so quietly?

In kindergarten, when Oy had first come to America, she hadn't spoken any English

75

and no kids had wanted to play with her. She remembered sitting just like that—still and all tucked in—on the floor of the classroom.

Or was it more than the phone call that had upset Liliandra? Oy thought of her dad's picture face-down on the table. She thought of Liliandra alone in the house at night.

Oy slipped off her perch, marched down the steps and across the rectangle of grass. She left the bright sunlight and entered the shadow of the ramada, lowering herself to sit beside Liliandra, so close that their shoulders touched.

"Hey," Oy said softly. "I didn't mean to hurt your feelings."

Liliandra tucked her head in tighter.

Oy went on: "I'm just trying to make everyone happy."

"Well, you didn't make *me* happy, that's for sure." Liliandra kept her head down, and the words, spoken against her knees, came out mumbly.

"*You* can still dance, though."

"By myself? Don't be crazy." Liliandra began to rock from side to side, one knee shifting up, then the other. She lifted her mouth an inch off her knee. "I don't want to do stuff by myself. I want to be with other kids."

Oy pulled up her own knees and hugged them tight.

Frankie's team ran by, scuffing the dust.

Liliandra suddenly stretched her legs out in front of her and sat very straight. "By the way, you're not in the Quail Club anymore."

"Oh!" was all that Oy could say. She felt like she had the time the tetherball smacked her in the chest. "But . . ."

"No *but*s. I made the rules really clear."

It was Oy's turn to put her head down on her knees.

77

❖ ELEVEN ❖

On Saturdays, Pak let the young Mexican man run the auto-parts store while she gave Oy her dance lesson.

Today, Pak was finishing up with a customer, and Oy waited on a metal stool in the back room. In the heat, the air smelled extra strong of the cardboard boxes stacked on the floor and of the car oil that leaked slowly from a punctured can. A small Buddha sat on a shelf along with a vase of silk flowers.

Oy pulled at the cuffs of her blouse, as though by covering her hands she could hide her troubles.

All day long, Pak sold auto parts to Americans. She lived in the real America. Maybe she could understand Oy's problem with Liliandra.

Just then, Pak came in, slamming the stockroom door behind her, her face flushed from hurrying. She wore yellowy gold jewelry from Thailand. Her mouth was outlined crisply with red lipstick.

"Sawasdee." Oy pressed her hands together and bowed to Pak. Instead of sitting up straight again, she kept looking down. Her lower lip trembled, and she bit it to keep from crying.

"What's wrong, Oy?" Pak asked.

Oy hesitated, biting her lip again, harder this time. Could she trust Pak? "It's that . . ." she began, then burst into tears.

Pak sat down on a nearby crate full of windshield wiper motors. She handed Oy a clump of tissues from her pocket.

When Oy had stopped crying, she told about Liliandra and the American dance.

Pak laughed at Oy's description of the dancing Americans on TV, throwing her head back so that her earrings tinkled.

"So Pak, I decided that I can't do the dance with Liliandra, and she got me thrown out of the Quail Club." Oy started to cry again.

"Quail Club?" Pak asked, raising her thin eyebrows.

Oy told her about the special invitation, about the coconut ice cream, about the incubator and Yuri, about the hatching.

Pak laughed again when Oy described the way the chicks held their beaks open waiting for a dropper of food. "So your girlfriend said you can't be in this club?" she asked when Oy finished.

Oy nodded.

"That's not a kind friend."

"But Pak, you don't understand—" Oy stopped, then went on: "I think I hurt Liliandra's feelings. Even though she was bossy, she was excited about having me do the dance. I didn't want to make her unhappy."

"Hmmm," said Pak. "It seems like there's no easy answer."

"No." Oy tore at the tissues in her hands.

"What do *you* want to do, Oy?" Pak asked.

Oy sniffed a big sniff, then sneezed and had to blow her nose. What *did* she want? She'd thought a lot about keeping others happy. "I'm not sure," she said.

"Close your eyes and try to figure it out."

81

She shut her eyes, then opened them. "I just don't know. . . ."

Pak gestured toward the small statue on the shelf. "The Buddha taught us to be kind to everyone, no matter how they act."

Oy sniffed and nodded, but she still felt confused. "How can I be kind to Liliandra and to Kun Mere and to myself all at the same time?"

"Close your eyes again, Oy."

Oy shut her eyes. After a moment, she said, "I want to be in the talent show with Liliandra. And I want to do my Thai dance. But Pak"—she opened her eyes wide—"those two things don't go together!"

Pak reached over and dabbed at Oy's face with a tissue. "Why not? Why don't you invite Liliandra to dance with you? She could dance the Thai Chicken Dance. It's an easy dance. Why don't you bring her here next time? I could teach her."

"But Pak—Liliandra isn't Thai," Oy said.

"Does she have two arms and two legs?"

Oy giggled and almost sneezed again. The metal stool rocked underneath her.

"Then she can still learn."

"But Pak, Liliandra is so mean. You said so yourself."

Pak handed Oy a fresh tissue. "Usually people are unkind when they are unhappy."

Oy stared at the smooth sheet of the tissue. The scent of Pak's tangy perfume, like lemons and jasmine flowers mixed together, swept over her. She remembered how sad and unkind Liliandra had been on the playground. She said slowly, "I think you're right, Pak."

Pak stood up and began to hunt through a

box of CDs, clacking them against one another. "Let's practice your dancing now."

Pak turned on the soft music with its bells like water gently running downhill. The auto-parts storage room was transformed into a stage. Oy forgot Liliandra. She pretended she was about to dance at Songkran, the white petal of the spotlight following her.

She began to cross the narrow space between the boxes, slowly moving her arms up and down as though she were flying. But instead of a chicken, Oy made believe that she was a quail. Even if she wasn't a member of the club anymore, she had seen the chicks hatch. If Pak's idea worked, maybe Liliandra would let her back in.

❖ TWELVE ❖

On Monday morning, Oy overheard Hejski and Marisa talking about the quail.

"When can we let them out of the cage?" Marisa wanted to know.

"Not for a while. Something might swoop down and eat them," Hejski said.

Oy left her spot in line and moved to the back. She couldn't bear to hear about the quail. They'd moved out of the warm safety of the incubator. They lived in a cage—a growing-up place—and she hadn't been there to see!

She imagined walking over to Hejski and saying *Liliandra says I'm not in the club anymore. Is that true? Can I be in anyway?* But the club was Liliandra's, even though it was held at Hejski's house.

Oy patted her shirt pocket and felt the crinkle of the plastic bag. The night before, she'd asked Kun Mere for a stamp from Kun Ya's last letter from Thailand. A Thai stamp for Liliandra's collection might make Liliandra listen to her.

When the line broke apart on the playground, Oy caught up with Liliandra. "I have something for you," she called. She crossed the fingers on both hands. Would one stamp be important enough to get Liliandra's attention?

Liliandra stopped, and Oy pulled the plastic bag from her pocket. Inside was the tiny square of paper.

Liliandra leaned closer. "Hey, that's the guy I saw on your wall. The king guy."

The king's portrait was on the stamp from Kun Ya's letter.

"It's for you. It's from Thailand."

"Thanks." Liliandra took the small package and shoved it into the pocket of her jeans. With one foot, then the other, she scuffed at the dandelions in the lawn.

"Let's sit here for a minute," Oy said.

"Do you have another stamp for me? Maybe the queen?"

"No, but I have something to ask you."

Liliandra plunked herself down on top of the dandelions.

Oy picked one. The milky sap ran down her thumb. She stared into the yellow face. "Liliandra, you know I just can't do the

American dance with you. It's too . . ." In her mind she thought *too American,* but she couldn't say that.

Liliandra opened her brown eyes wide, then narrowed them.

"I have another idea though," Oy said quickly. "Do you want to dance with *me?* The Thai dance? We could do it together."

Liliandra wrinkled her nose.

"The dance isn't hard. My teacher will teach you."

Liliandra didn't say anything. She began to tear the fringe of petals off a dandelion.

Oy sighed. The plan wasn't going to work.

An airplane crossed the sky with a bright roar. Oy glanced up to see the vapor trail spreading, tight and neat in the airplane's path, then pluming out in the distance. She wished she were in that plane, traveling to

Thailand instead of sitting here, trying to make everything come out right.

Oy tried again. "In Thailand, girls don't dance in tank tops and jeans. They wear lots of gold jewelry and special dresses like my pink one. My dancing teacher knows where to get the material. We could look really pretty, like princesses."

"Naw. I don't want to do anything weird."

"Thai dancing isn't weird," Oy said. "It's pretty."

"It's weird to me. I've never seen it. I bet it isn't even on cable." Liliandra uncrossed her legs and extended them into the dandelions.

Like Liliandra, Oy began to tear the petals off her dandelion. No talent show could be worth this much trouble.

❖ ❖ ❖

After school, Oy walked with Frankie as far as Jerry's Lee Ho Market.

A line of palm trees cast shadows over the street, and a rough little wind stirred the dust.

"So what have you decided about the talent show?" Frankie asked.

"I may not do anything," she surprised herself by saying. "I may not be in it after all."

"How come?"

"It's not fun anymore." She kicked a round pebble so that it rolled ahead of them, clattering along.

"I see you with Liliandra a lot," Frankie said. "But I hardly see you practice. It always looks like you're having a fight."

Oy's chin trembled, and she wiped her eyes with the back of her hand. "Liliandra says I can't be in the Quail Club."

"I'm sorry, Oy," Frankie said.

She turned her face away from him and pretended to cough.

They walked on in silence except for the rhythmic crunch of their shoes on the gravel.

Suddenly, Oy couldn't go on. She plunked herself down on the hard concrete of the curb, pressed her face into her hands, and cried.

Frankie sat beside her, so close that his backpack touched hers. After a while, he said, "I've known Liliandra since kindergarten. She's hard to get along with. She's really mean and tricky."

"I know," Oy said, staring into the gutter at an old gum wrapper, a twig, and pebbles caught in a swirl of mud.

Frankie picked up the twig and flicked at the pebbles.

It felt good to be next to Frankie, not

having to say anything. The two sat together until the shadow of a palm tree climbed over their legs.

Finally, Oy stood up.

"Do you want to stop in the store for a soda?" Frankie asked. "An ice-cream bar?"

"No, thank you. I'm late and had better get home. My mother will worry about me."

"Oy." He faced her, the tuft of his hair lifted by the breeze. "Forget what Liliandra wants. Just do your own thing."

That night, Oy was playing a game of cards with Luk.

"Do you have a tiger?" Luk asked in English.

"No, Luk. Go fish."

The phone rang.

Luk ran to answer. "It's your friend," she

said, handing the receiver to Oy. "It's Kelly Marie."

Oy held up one finger to let Luk know she'd be right back, then carried the phone into her room.

"Where have you been?" Kelly Marie wanted to know. "We had a Quail Club meeting and you weren't there. The quail are running around and they eat all by themselves."

Oy sat down at her desk. With one hand, she shuffled her school papers into a pile. "I can't come anymore."

"Why not?"

Oy swallowed hard. "Liliandra says I can't."

"Why not?" Kelly Marie asked again.

"Because I won't dance with her."

"Oh, yeah?"

Oy waited for Kelly Marie to say, *That's silly. Come anyway.* But she didn't.

Instead, she said, "Maybe Liliandra will change her mind."

But Liliandra wouldn't.

After Oy and Kelly Marie had said goodbye, Oy tapped a pencil against the edge of the desk.

Luk peeked in the door.

Oy held up one finger again. "Another minute, Luk."

She had to get back in the Quail Club. Liliandra had to see pretty Thai dancing.

There was just one possibility.

Oy tapped the pencil faster.

What if Liliandra said no? She'd already said no once.

Oy thought of what Kelly Marie had said about the quail chicks running and eating. She laid down the pencil, opened the tiny green phone book, and dialed Liliandra's number.

The phone rang once and Liliandra answered.

"Liliandra?" Oy asked.

"Oh, hey there."

Oy fixed her eyes on a poster of Thai fruits that hung above her bed, each one exotic and delicious. "Liliandra, there's a cool Thai party in a few days. I'm going to dance. You could come and see Thai dancing for yourself."

"Will there be candy?"

"Probably. And music. It's a festival where everyone gets wet. There will be water fights."

"Water fights?"

"To remind the spirits to send rain for the crops."

"What?" Liliandra asked loudly.

"Never mind. The water fights are just fun, that's all. Can you come?" As she waited, she silently named the fruits: *mangosteen, finger bananas, jackfruit* . . .

"Maybe. But I don't want to be the only white person there."

"There will be hundreds of *farangs* coming from all over the city."

"Fa-what?"

"*Farangs*. It means people who aren't Thai." *Rambutan, star fruit, longan . . .*

"I don't know. It might be too weird. And my mom doesn't like to drive me places."

"What if my dad picked you up?" *Mango, lychee . . .* The late afternoon sunlight fell through the open window, making a square of light on the desk.

"I guess."

"Oh, good," Oy said happily. She'd done it. Liliandra had said yes. Oy could taste the sweetness of each fruit she'd named. The sunlight on her desk was as yellow as the gold of Thai jewelry.

Luk pushed open the door again. This time she held the pack of cards. "Go fish?"

Oy nodded. "Yes, Luk. Let's play."

❖ THIRTEEN ❖

On the morning of Thai New Year, Oy and Kun Mere shook out the floor mats, swept every room in the house, and washed the windows.

Luk helped Kun Pa clean the rust-colored station wagon.

It was a New Year's cleaning, clearing away all the sadness and bad actions of the previous year. It was supposed to be a happy time.

Yet as Oy polished one side of the kitchen window while Kun Mere polished the other, their cloths on opposite sides of the glass, Oy kept polishing even after her side was dry.

Kun Mere slid the window open. "Are you worried again, little daughter?" she asked.

Oy crumpled the paper towel in her fist. "I don't know if my friend will like Songkran."

"Of course she will. Everyone likes Thai New Year." Kun Mere closed the window again.

Oy wasn't so sure. She watched Kun Pa lift the Buddha from his place on the altar in the living room.

The statue was made of wood and was about two feet high. The Buddha sat with his eyes half closed and his palms held open.

Kun Mere gently wiped him with a damp cloth, then Kun Pa carried him to the station wagon and set him on a silk pillow in the front seat.

In Thailand, people took their Buddha statues out on Songkran to see Thai New Year and to receive blessings of water.

Riding to Liliandra's, Kun Mere put her hand on the Buddha to keep him from toppling over.

When they picked up Liliandra, she came out of her yellow house carrying a paper bag. She closed the front gate behind her, walked toward the car, then stopped. She pointed at the Buddha: "What's that—I can't remember his name—doing in the front seat?"

Now Oy saw that taking the Buddha in the car was a strange, un-American thing. She smiled and waved her hand as though having a statue in the front seat was normal. "He's just going for a ride."

Liliandra climbed in and slammed the door. "Hmm." She set the paper bag beside her on the seat.

"What's in your bag?" Oy asked.

"It's my food," she said. "Just in case."

Oy stared at the bag, at its texture of brown wrinkles. What if Liliandra *didn't* like the Thai food? What if she didn't like the festival at all? She thought of the way Liliandra had pinched her nose at the smell of durian. Worst of all, what if Liliandra said something about Songkran that made Oy not like the festival herself?

Kun Pa drove to a community center in the neighborhood near the temple. The temple itself was too small to hold all the *farangs* who would come to Songkran.

Inside the hall, the golden temple Buddha was already in his place on the stage. Pak and other women were decorating him with a length of yellow cloth and garlands of flowers. Candles and sticks of incense burned at his large feet.

"Wow," said Liliandra. "That is so cool. That is like a big one of yours."

Other families had also brought their household Buddhas. Some were as small as thimbles, others large; some were tall and slender with pointy headdresses. Some Buddhas were made of wood; others were painted gold. Two were of green jade and one was of red stone.

Liliandra leaned forward against the stage, gazing at the Buddhas one by one.

So far, so good, Oy thought.

Kun Pa set the Buddha next to the others.

Oy took a lotus flower from Pak's pile and placed it at the Buddha's feet for luck. She needed luck.

Five monks sat in a row behind the Buddhas, their orange robes glowing in the gloom of the unlit stage.

"Those guys look like Buddhas that are alive," Liliandra said.

Oy smiled. "That's what they're trying to be."

"Good morning, girls." It was Pak, wearing her own gold-threaded dress, cherry-colored and flashy in the dim light.

Oy pressed her palms together and bowed slightly to her. "Teacher, this is my friend, Liliandra." She hoped that Pak wouldn't mention the Thai dancing. Not yet.

"Pleased to meet you," Pak said.

Liliandra extended a hand, as though to touch Pak's dress. Then she glanced at Oy and bowed to Pak, her hands folded neatly in front of her.

Pak gave a little laugh. "You two can help with this," she said. She gestured toward a silver bowl filled with water and then to a pile of jasmine flowers and stalks of lemon grass. "We need to scent the water."

"Oooh, I get to do something too?" Liliandra asked.

"Of course. Here," said Pak, "break these jasmine flowers off the stems so they can float."

As Liliandra began to work, she whispered, "These smell so pretty."

Oy cut the lemon grass into small pieces.

"Hey, what are these?" Liliandra touched a tub of water balloons under the table.

"You'll see." When Liliandra wasn't looking, Oy used her foot to push the tub farther under the table. The balloons were for later, outside on the lawn. No one ever threw them inside.

"Hey!" Liliandra shouted suddenly, dropping her stem of jasmine.

Oy turned to see Luk with a water pistol.

She'd shot Liliandra in the back. Luk giggled and ran.

"I told you you'd get wet," Oy said, hoping that Liliandra wasn't mad.

"Okay," said Liliandra, bending down to the tub of water balloons. She picked up one and hurled it at Luk. It broke with a loud *splat*.

Oy looked around quickly. No one seemed to have noticed.

Kun Pa busily helped the men unload folding chairs and cases of soda.

Kun Mere talked and laughed and chopped vegetables in the kitchen.

What was Liliandra thinking? No one was supposed to get wild now. Not *yet*. The water balloons weren't for in *here*.

"That'll teach your sister a lesson," Liliandra said, and went back to her job with the flowers.

As Oy sliced each stalk, she told herself that Liliandra didn't know about the water balloons. She hadn't meant to do anything wrong. Not really.

When Oy had a neat pile of lemon grass, and Liliandra one of blossoms, they lowered their piles into the bowl of water.

"Soon the water will smell sweet," Oy said.

"Just like perfume," Liliandra said. Then she turned and pointed to the monks. "Why do *they* get lunch early?"

Women were carrying plates to the stage and spreading the food on mats in front of the monks.

"The monks can't eat after twelve o'clock," Oy explained.

"Like my mom when she's on a diet."

"No, it's not a diet. They give up dinner so they won't be greedy."

Liliandra raised an eyebrow.

After the monks had eaten and their dishes were cleared away, they began to chant. Everyone except for Liliandra was too busy to stop and listen.

Liliandra perched on the edge of the stage and stared at the monks. She swayed her body slightly to the rhythm.

Oy smiled again.

When the chanting was finished, the monks walked off the stage and formed a line in front of the row of Buddhas. They dipped the silver cup into the scented water that Oy and Liliandra had prepared. One by one, they poured water over the head and shoulders of each Buddha.

"Why are they doing that? Why are they getting them all wet?" Liliandra asked.

"Shhh. Not so loud. The water is a blessing. Besides, it's hot in Thailand in April, and everyone wants to cool down."

"Even the Buddha?"

"Even him."

"Now we do the same thing," Oy said

106

when the monks had finished and everyone else was lining up.

"Me too?"

"Yes. You make a wish as you pour the water."

"Can I wish for anything I want?"

"Of course," Oy said.

When it came her turn to pour, the sweet water splashing lightly over one Buddha after another, Oy wished that Liliandra would love the festival. Love it enough to want to do the Thai dance. Love the Thai dance and invite her back into the Quail Club.

While Liliandra poured, Oy watched her face, trying to guess her wish. Could she be wishing that Oy would do the American dance with her after all? Could she—Oy sucked in her breath—could she be wishing that Oy would be her friend?

As Liliandra handed the cup to Luk, she smiled.

The monks went out into the crowd, mingling with people, joking and talking.

Dancers entered the hall, carrying costumes over their shoulders in garment bags.

A band set up onstage, replacing the sound of the monks' chanting with the warm-up sounds of guitars and keyboard. When the young men started to play, the music was jingly and fast, like a mix of Thai and American music.

In a corner at the back of the room, Liliandra started to dance. "Come on, Olivia. You can dance too."

Oy stood behind Liliandra and moved the way she moved, but her movements were smaller than Liliandra's. She looked around to see if anyone was watching.

The *farangs* arrived, buying their tickets at

the door; they carried paper plates of fragrant *satay* chicken, pineapple fried rice, and *pad Thai* noodles to the tables to eat.

Kun Pa took the tub of water balloons outside, and Oy heard the shrieks of a water-balloon fight. Kids chased each other through the hall with water pistols.

In the kitchen, the women, squealing, tossed cups of water back and forth at each other.

The *farangs* stared.

Liliandra disappeared.

Oy found her outside holding a load of water balloons in the crook of one arm.

"This is the best part!" Liliandra called across the lawn, then threw a balloon straight at Oy.

The water hit Oy in the chest and splashed up to her face.

It was a cold surprise and the blow stung. It was as though Liliandra was telling her again that she wasn't in the Quail Club. Oy picked up a water balloon from the tub and bent her arm to throw it—not in a playful Songkran way—but as if she was in a real fight. Her arm was hot with anger. She didn't care if Liliandra's father *was* away all the time. She didn't care if Liliandra was alone in the dark house. Or if she didn't have a real friend. It was too hard watching Liliandra and hoping she was having fun and hoping that she wouldn't get anyone upset. And now Oy's blouse was all wet.

Oy hurled the balloon.

It broke at Liliandra's feet, getting her plastic flip-flops wet.

Liliandra shrieked.

"Serves you right!" Oy shouted.

Liliandra threw another balloon at Oy, but it landed in the bushes.

Pak touched Oy's shoulder. "It's time to get ready," she said quietly. "Bring your friend."

Oy felt Pak's hand laid calmly on her shoulder. She smelled her lemony perfume. She looked at Liliandra, who was shaking the water off her shoes, standing first on one foot, then the other.

Liliandra had just been having fun with the water balloon.

"Do you want to watch me and the other dancers get dressed?" Oy called out.

Liliandra looked around.

The water fight had moved to the other side of the grass. No one dared wet Pak in her cherry-colored costume.

"I guess," she said.

Dripping wet, Oy led Liliandra into the bathroom, where the mirrors had round bulbs around the edges. The room smelled of perfume and face powder and was filled with women and girls dressing, leaning close to the mirrors to put on makeup and fluffy fake eyelashes. A girl in an iridescent dress, like a fabric of captured rainbows, helped a woman in glossy satin clasp her gold necklace. Another put on sparkling earrings. A teenage girl with a crown of flowers bent down to fasten ankle bracelets with tinkly bells.

Everywhere gold-threaded fabric shone like the sun.

Liliandra watched, her eyes growing wider and wider.

Oy slipped off her shorts and stepped into her skirt.

Pak helped Oy hook the skirt. She pinned the sashes, holding several small gold pins between her teeth.

She painted red lipstick on Oy's lips and dabbed her cheeks with brushfuls of pink powder. She brushed Oy's hair to the top of her head and secured it with a gold crown.

Liliandra pointed to the crown. "Can I touch it?"

Oy felt Liliandra's fingers lightly stroke the lacy gold. Her touch was gentle, and Oy felt as if Liliandra was touching *her*. Liliandra hadn't meant to hurt her with the water balloon.

Finally, Pak opened a box. Inside was a set of long golden fingernails.

"I'm doing the fingernail dance," Oy explained to Liliandra.

"But those are humongous." Liliandra bent over the box. "Even longer than my mom's."

One by one, Pak placed the fingernails on Oy's fingers.

By the last finger, Liliandra's mouth had dropped open.

❖ ❖ ❖

The program started with Thai sword fighting. While the band played cool, sad music, the sword fighters bowed to each other and to the Buddhas, pressing their foreheads to the ground.

Suddenly, they leaped up and began to fight ferociously, dancing across the stage, their swords clattering, clouds of orange sparks flying.

"Oh, man! They're gonna chop each other's heads off!" Liliandra shouted.

"They want to scare us," Oy said. "But really, they won't hurt each other." Even so, she shuddered whenever the swords clanked together. She thought of the feeling in her arm when she'd thrown the balloon at Liliandra.

After the sword fighters had finished— neither hurt—they bowed to the audience and left the stage.

It was Oy's turn to dance.

As the music began and Oy moved into

the spotlight, she noticed Liliandra watching from the edge of the stage, tucked between the velvet curtains.

She made her arms soft. Pak said they needed to feel like underwater plants waving in a current. She dipped low when she bent her knees. She showed off the long fingernails, her hands heavy with gold.

Oy wanted to dance well for the Thai people in the audience, to remind them of home. She danced to remind the spirits to send water for the crops. And she was dancing so that Liliandra would love the dance, would want to do Thai dancing herself.

When the music ended quietly, slipping into silence, Oy stood for a moment with her hands pressed together, the long fingernails shining, while the audience clapped for her.

Then she left the stage, exiting into the dark wings, where Liliandra was waiting.

"If I danced with you, could I use those awesome fingernails?"

Was Liliandra changing her mind? Oy studied her face in the dim light, then shook her head. "The fingernail dance is too hard if you're just beginning. We could do the Chicken Dance."

Liliandra wrinkled her nose as though she was smelling durian again.

"We could pretend that we're quail instead," Oy said quickly. Then she bit her bottom lip. She hadn't meant to say the word *quail*. She was hoping that Liliandra would bring up the Quail Club first. But now the word was out.

The velvet curtain was soft against her bare shoulder. She stood very still, waiting for Liliandra to say something about quail, the Quail Club.

Onstage, two men held two bamboo poles

116

close to the ground and began to knock them together and apart as dancers danced in and out of the space in between. The dancers were accompanied by a drum and the shaking sounds of the *ungaloong.*

"That is totally awesome," Liliandra said. "But I wouldn't want to get *my* legs caught by those sticks."

Liliandra watched the dance, and Oy watched Liliandra, holding her breath. Now— *now* was the perfect moment. Her costume suddenly felt tight and itchy. The jewelry pinched.

And then Liliandra turned and said to Oy, "Okay. I'll dance with you."

Oy rose up on her tiptoes and back down again, the bells on her ankle bracelets ringing. *Oh, yes!*

"And I'll let you back in the club, but only on one condition."

Oy froze. "What is that?" Her voice sounded tiny, like the high-pitched little wind chime in Kun Mere's garden. What more could Liliandra ask?

"When we practice with your teacher—I get to wear your pink dress."

Her pink dress. How could Liliandra ask for *that*? Last year, Liliandra had persuaded Oy to bring the dress to school. She'd tried it on and so had other girls. The precious pink silk had gotten dirty and torn.

And now Liliandra was asking for the dress again.

Oy looked at the women dancing in and out of the shifting bamboo poles. One false move and they'd trip and fall. They might even hurt themselves. Yet they'd chosen to perform the risky dance and were all smiling bravely.

Oy turned back to Liliandra. "Okay. It's a deal."

❖ FOURTEEN ❖

"This doesn't look like a dance studio," said Liliandra when Kun Pa dropped them off at Pak's for Liliandra's first dance lesson. "This is where they sell car stuff. When my uncle fixes his car, he comes here."

Pak was at the cash register, partly hidden by a display of tire gauges, and wearing a blouse of slippery Thai silk and a pendent with a portrait of the king of Thailand on it.

"That's him again," Liliandra whispered, leaning close to Oy. "The king."

Pak came out from behind the counter. She put her hands on her hips and looked Liliandra up and down, the corners of her red lips turning up in a smile.

Liliandra wore overalls, with one strap undone. Her hair fell loose over her shoulders.

"First of all, you will feel more Thai if you look more Thai," Pak said.

Taking a comb from her purse, she combed Liliandra's hair up into a ponytail on top of her head, then twisted the ponytail into a bun and ran a pencil through to hold it.

Pak knew just what to do, Oy thought.

Pak stood back to look. "From the audience, no one will know you're not Thai," she assured Liliandra.

"Where's the mirror?" Liliandra asked, glancing down the aisle that said MIRRORS, TIRE FLAPS, AND OTHER ACCESSORIES.

"Come with me." Oy beckoned. She took

Liliandra through the store to Pak's back room and into a tiny bathroom.

The sink was scummy with car grease, and the room held crates of seat covers, but Liliandra didn't seem to notice. She leaned over the dirty sink and examined herself in the mirror. "The hairdo is okay," she finally said, "but where's the dress?"

Oy pulled it out of her backpack. The glittery, cool fabric gleamed in the plastic bag. The year before, with Kun Mere's help, Oy had washed and mended the dress after Liliandra had treated it roughly. For that, it was all the more precious to her now.

Oy handed the bag over to Liliandra.

Liliandra's eyes widened. She slipped her hand under the plastic and touched the dress. She took it out of the plastic bag and pressed it to her cheek. "Oh, it feels so pretty."

"And now?" Oy asked.

121

"I'll tell Hejski to let you back in."

"Okay." Partly Oy felt like crushing Liliandra in a big hug, and partly she felt like throwing a water balloon at her. She kept her fingers crossed behind her back. Who knew what Liliandra would do next?

Pak knocked and entered the bathroom.

Liliandra held Oy's skirt up to her waist.

"I'm letting her use my dress," Oy announced.

"So I see. Do you need help to put it on, little daughter?"

Oy waited in the back room while Pak dressed Liliandra. This time, Pak would make sure that Lilandra treated the dress carefully. Oy made up a little game with the floor tiles, jumping from one to the next, each time rhyming with *quail: rail, tail, bale* . . .

The bathroom door opened and Liliandra

stepped out, saying, "I do look like a princess. I really do."

Pak had put the dress on just right.

"You look pretty, Liliandra," Oy said. Seeing Liliandra dressed like a Thai girl was almost like looking at herself.

"Very nice," Pak said. "Now I have two Thai chickens."

"Quail," Liliandra whispered when Pak turned around to push the button on the CD player.

"Yes, quail," Oy repeated.

❖ FIFTEEN ❖

The next meeting of the Quail Club was held the following afternoon.

Yuri picked the girls up from school and drove them home with all the windows open, the warm air pulsing through the car.

Oy felt her hair blowing back from her face, and Kelly Marie and Marisa's shoulders pressing against her own. Yuri had handed out candy, and the soft caramel melted in Oy's mouth. Her heart sang a thuddity little song. She was with her friends again and on the way to the quail.

At Hejski's, everyone jumped out of the car and hurried along the round patio stones by the side of the garage.

The cage was set under a tree with long drooping branches. Although the quail huddled together, the enclosure was large enough for them to run freely.

Oy knelt down beside the cage.

Oh, how the chicks had grown! They looked less like the pompoms on Marisa's shoelaces—their fluffy down had turned to speckled brown feathers.

Marisa snapped more photos.

After consulting her book, Hejski announced, "Today we can hold them." She unlatched the door of the cage, reached in, and picked up the nearest quail.

Oy held out her hands, and Hejski placed the chick in the hollow of her palms.

The quail was warm and light and fragile. Oy closed both hands over it, feeling the delicate scratches of the feet against her fingers.

Hejski handed quail to Kelly Marie, Marisa, and Liliandra.

When Hejski came with an eyedropper of food, Oy opened her hands some to let Hejski tilt the food into the bird's beak. The quail chick gulped and swallowed and was ready for more.

Oy sat down with her treasure. She peeked into her hands at the small bird and sighed. She'd come so close to not having this moment.

"That's enough," said Hejski. She took the birds back to the cage one by one, coming for Oy's at the very end.

Yuri brought out a carton of chocolate

milk, a box of round crackers, and orange Cheez-ee Delite that squirted from a can. Kun Mere would have frowned at Cheez-ee Delite. She wouldn't have let that fake American stuff into the house.

Oy wiped her hands with one of the towelettes that Hejski offered, and sat down with the others around the table.

"Olivia gave me a stamp from Thailand," Liliandra announced. "She also took me to a Thailand New Year's party. Plus we're doing that Thailand dance."

"You're doing it *together*?" Marisa stared at Liliandra, then at Oy.

Oy nodded. Liliandra made it sound so simple.

"Yup," Liliandra said. "We're gonna wear those pretty Thailand dresses."

"Ooh, la-la," said Hejski.

Kelly Marie giggled.

Oy helped herself to five crackers, looking down into the box so the girls wouldn't see her big smile. While Liliandra had made her a little more American, Oy had made Liliandra a little bit Thai.

"It's time to name the quail," said Hejski.

"I'm going to let Olivia name mine," Liliandra said. "Mine will have Thailand names."

"Olivia should give hers Thailand names too," said Marisa, popping a white cracker into her mouth.

"Mine will have plain old American names," said Kelly Marie. "*George* and *Elizabeth*."

"And I'll do names from Finland," Hejski said.

"Like *Yuri*," said Kelly Marie.

With her mouth full of cracker, Marisa said, "Then mine will be *Chiquita* and *Pajarito*."

Oy took a sip of chocolate milk and waited for the Cheez-ee Delite to come her way.

128

The girls were just playing with the idea of being from other countries. While their parents had come from Finland or Mexico, the girls always thought of themselves as Americans. Oy had been in the U.S. since kindergarten. Wasn't it time to think of herself as American too?

The can of cheese arrived, and Oy squirted big dollops onto her crackers. "I'm going to call one of my quail *Nok Noi*. That means 'little bird.' But I want to give the other an American name—something like *Nancy* or *Andy*." She licked the orange cheese. "One should have an American name because I'm a Thai American."

❖ SIXTEEN ❖

The big night had finally come. A banner hung in the auditorium with THE TALENT SHOW written in sparkly letters.

Oy and Liliandra got dressed in the room behind the stage. Liliandra had a green gold-threaded dress that Pak had sewn for her. They helped each other pin the sashes.

There hadn't been enough time to get Liliandra jewelry from Thailand.

"You can wear half of mine," Oy said, handing Liliandra a gold necklace decorated with rubies and emeralds.

"I want to wear the gold crown," Liliandra announced.

Oy held the crown in her palm. It was her favorite piece of jewelry, but she could wear it anytime. "Here, then." She offered Liliandra the circle of gold.

Liliandra's hand darted out, then stopped just before she touched the crown. She sighed, then looked at Oy. "No, you should have it."

Their eyes met, and Liliandra was the first to look away.

Oy lifted the crown onto her topknot of hair before Liliandra could change her mind.

When they went out to the courtyard, where the other performers were gathered, Marisa held up her camera and snapped a photo of them, the flash lighting up the trees.

"Oooh, so pretty," said Kelly Marie.

Oy heard a whistle and saw Frankie running through the shadows.

Marisa and Kelly Marie were dressed in matching red, white, and blue outfits, ready to sing "America the Beautiful."

"I thought you didn't like being onstage," Oy said to Marisa.

Marisa shrugged. "Things change."

"Come look," said Kelly Marie. She led the others to the back of the auditorium. Right where people came in hung the Quail Club poster.

Oy had helped glue Marisa's photos in rows onto the poster board, and she'd written the captions underneath them in her nice handwriting. She'd done the captions not only in English, but in the fancy swirls of the Thai alphabet as well.

"That looks so cool," Liliandra said.

The principal came onstage with a microphone and announced that the talent show was beginning.

Everyone ran to the lunch courtyard, Oy and Liliandra at the back, taking small steps in their tight skirts.

The Quail Dance was the second act up. Waiting in the wings, Oy watched three girls skipping rope onstage and her own heart beat fast, as if she too were doing fancy tricks. She touched the tiny pins holding her pink sashes, making sure they were safely fastened.

Peeking out from behind the curtain toward the audience, Oy saw only darkness at first. But as her eyes adjusted, she made out Mrs. Danovitch sitting very tall in the front row, holding her white program. Nearby sat Frankie and Hejski, whose cousin hadn't gotten married after all. Next to them, Luk perched on Kun Pa's lap. Kun Mere and Pak were easy to see. They had on their own gold-threaded dresses—Kun Mere's sky blue and Pak's cherry-colored. The threads gleamed in the dark auditorium. How beautiful they look, Oy thought, like two jewels in the ocean of people in ordinary clothes.

"There's my mom!" Liliandra said loudly, pointing to a dark-haired woman on the other side of Mrs. Danovitch.

The skipping act ended. Clapping began, peaked, and died away to whispers and rustling.

The music for the Quail Dance started, filling the auditorium with a cascade of xylophone notes.

Oy stepped out, moving gracefully into the overlapping pools of pink light. When the *clui* flute joined the xylophone, she lifted her arms and let them float down, a bird flying in slow motion.

As she danced, she sensed her friend, lover of crazy American TV dancing, moving softly and deliberately beside her.

GLOSSARY

chiquita: (Spanish) little one (feminine form)

clui: Thai flute

durian: a tropical fruit with a hard, spiky exterior and custardlike interior

farang: (Thai) foreigner

ghler: (Thai) strongly bonded friends

jackfruit: a fruit with rubbery golden sections

krain jai: (Thai) manner of not offending others

Kun Loong: (Thai) Uncle

Kun Mere: (Thai) Mother

Kun Pa: (Thai) Father

Kun Ya: (Thai) Grandmother

longan: a fruit with a furry brown exterior and hard white flesh inside

lychee: a round white fruit with a tough brown skin

mangosteen: a fruit with a dark purple exterior and white segments inside

nok noi: (Thai) little bird

pad Thai: a noodle dish with vegetables and eggs

pajarito: (Spanish) little bird

rambutan: a small oval fruit with a red spiky exterior and hard white flesh inside

ranad: Thai xylophone

satay **chicken:** grilled skewered chicken, served with peanut sauce

sawasdee: (Thai) *hello* and *goodbye*

Songkran: Thai New Year

star fruit: a waxy yellow fruit

tom kha: (Thai) chicken-and-vegetable soup with coconut broth

ungaloong: Thai instrument that is shaken to produce sound

wat: Buddhist temple

A TALE OF SPIRITUAL AWAKENING

The Buddha's Diamonds
by Carolyn Marsden

Nothing makes Tinh feel prouder than his
family's new bamboo fishing boat. When a
terrible storm threatens his small Vietnamese
village, Tinh has to make sure the boat is
safe. But the wind and rain are frightening,
and Tinh must look inside himself, and to
the compassionate teachings of the Buddha,
to find the courage to save his beloved boat.

Hardcover ISBN 978-0-7636-3380-6

CANDLEWICK PRESS
www.candlewick.com

ALSO BY CAROLYN MARSDEN

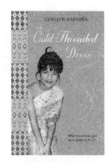

Hardcover
ISBN 978-0-7636-1569-7

Hardcover
ISBN 978-0-7636-2117-9

Hardcover
ISBN 978-0-7636-2257-2

Paperback
ISBN 978-0-7636-2993-9

Paperback
ISBN 978-0-7636-3304-2

Paperback
ISBN 978-0-7636-3376-9

*co-written with
Virginia Shin-Mui Loh*

Hardcover
ISBN 978-0-7636-3012-6

Hardcover
ISBN 978-0-7636-3175-8

CANDLEWICK PRESS
www.candlewick.com